Special thanks to our boys Chandler Carter, Tad Trimarco and Jon Trimarco
and to all our children at the Notable Kids Arts Center.
Your wisdom, curiosity, theatrics and pure joy inspire us everyday.
You're all just so...

it's just so...

written by Brenda Faatz & Peter Trimarco
illustrations by Peter Trimarco

Printed in the USA
Notable Kids Publishing • Colorado

As the sun peeked through in its glorious way
the bluebirds' song greeted Lizzy's big day.
She lay very still to catch some more Zzzzzzzzs
and did her best to NOT wake with ease.

It's just so......early!

Grumbly... Growly

her tummy made its plea,
"Time to leave the pillow
and get to feeding me!"

It's just so.....noisy!

For Lizzy's first day in a brand new school
she declared to her mom her new *fashion rule*.
"From this day forward," she did say
"I'll dress myself in my own Lizzy-way."

Dressed in her best with backpack in tow,
her tummy excited – BUT – should she go?
Would she make friends? Would she be all alone?
In truth Lizzy worried, a new school – the unknown!

It's just so...scary

She boarded the bus for the very first time
and felt oh-so-big as the stairs she did climb.

It's just so...tall

In front of the school, stood Lizzy in awe.
A building of humongous size she saw.
Inside there were teachers, books, pencils and fears.
She thought to run home as she fought back the tears.

It's just so.................

The bell rang for school
and time for a book,
which gave Lizzy's morning
a whole new look.

It's

just

so…

so

so

SO

SO

SO

SO

SOOOOOOOOOooo

OOOOOOOOOOOOOOOOOOOOOOOO **wordy.**

They read all the classics
from "Dick, Jane and Spot,"
to "Make Way for Ducklings"
and "Sir Lancelot."

Lizzy jumped on the desk
and surpised everyone,
acting out stories –
what crazy good fun!

It's just so…

…dramatical!

Lizzy faced what once scared her
and soon was amazed –
... addition ... subtraction
were all the new craze.

Using fingers and toes,
Lizzy would blossom.
She found that math
was really quite awesome.

Science was not as weird as she feared
with atoms now split and stars pioneered.
Beakers and test tubes with both hands she gripped.
The slime it did ooooze with a glub
...drip...drip...drip.

It's

just

so...

.....fizz-astro-fantastical

Plum-purple, berry-blue splashed everywhere.
She imagined in colors with bold Lizzy-flair.

Great care Lizzy took to paint outside the lines.
As a fierce crayon-artist she started to shine.

The first day of school had so far been fine.
But Lizzy knew no one – alone she would dine.

She ate by herself
with her PB & J

chip-CRUNCHING,

juice-SLURPING,

not a word did she say.

It's just so
lonely...

me only.

She got up the courage
to say "Hi" to a neighbor.
Soon chatter and giggles
gave lunch a new flavor.

She made ONE new friend,
then TWO... and then FOUR...
When others joined in
there were so many more.

It's just so...
crunch-muncha-licious

Back with full tummies and all wanting naps
their eyes popped wide open and gazed at cool maps.
Exploring the world with adventure and wonder
they learned about animals living down under.

Wombats, wallabies, freckled ducks, kangaroos
platypus, possum, and flightless emus –
Lizzy sprang to full dance, sea dragon style,
and wallaroo-wiggled with an ear-to-ear smile.

It's just so.....**Wombatty**

The day's book reading and science now done,
it came time for music – and Oh it was fun!

With a 'Do Re Mi Fa'
and a 'Fa So La Ti'
the children all sang
with laughter and glee.

It's just so...

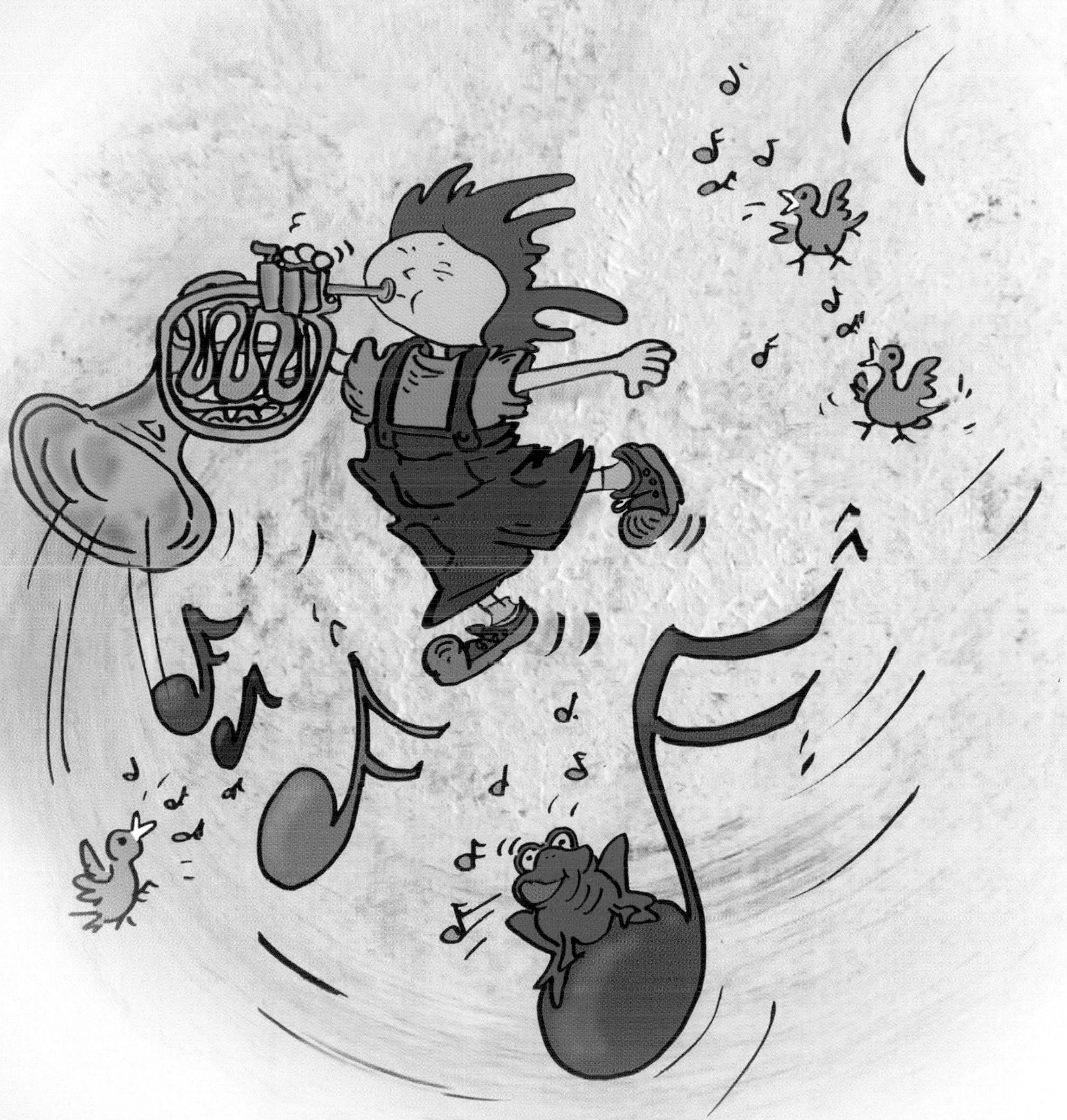

oompa-pa
chugga-doo-zippidy-la

The first day of school now a thing of the past,
books...crayons...beakers, it all went so fast.

With new friends and giggles – dwarf stars and the moon,
wild wallaroo-wiggles...the day ended too soon.

Now home among friends with so much to say,
Lizzy told one and all of her wombatty day
– of 'Do Re Mi Fa' and 'Fa So La Ti'
– of oookie glub-dripping
it's just so...

.....whooooooopeeeee!

When it came time for dinner excitement did swell,
with mom and dad waiting – more stories to tell.

It's just so...

fantastical explorational
science-sational
colorifical animalogical

epic.

Playtime long over
and dinner complete,
it came time for washing
ears, nose, knees and feet.

Bath water rumbled
and bubbles did rise,
as Lizzy would venture
through suds twice her size.

It's just so...

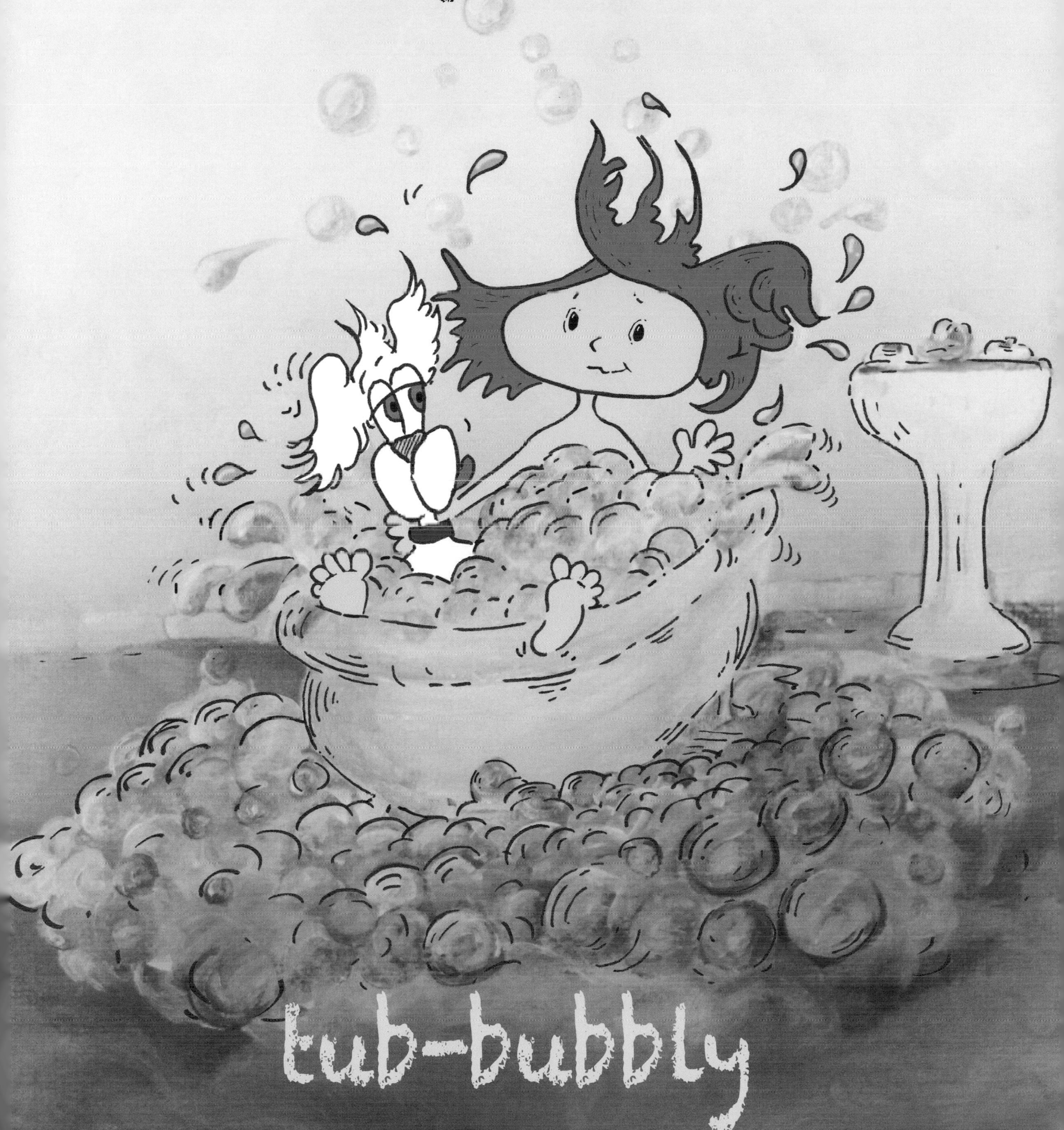

tub-bubbly

Soggy and sleepy, she shuffled to bed,
old worries and fears now out of her head.
She yawned for tonight and would dream of tomorrow.

But WAIT!
To sleep by herself?
This brought Lizzy such sorrow.

But something **fantastical** happened that night
when in through the window came friends – what a sight!
They crawled 'cross the floor as she started to snore.
Soon Lizzy was dreaming – and lonely no more.

It's
all
just...

...SO

Copyright ©2015 by Peter Trimarco and Brenda Faatz.
Lizzy Character ©2015 Faatz & Trimarco
All rights reserved. Published by Notable Kids Publishing, LLC.
No part of this publication may be reproduced in any form without written permission of the copyright owner or publisher.
For information write to Notable Kids Publishing, Box 2047, Parker, Colorado 80134

Library of Congress Control Number: 2 0 1 5 9 1 9 8 5 0
Faatz, Brenda
Trimarco,Peter
It's Just So... / written by Brenda Faatz / Peter Trimarco and illustrated by Peter Trimarco – 1st ed.
Summary: Things can sometimes seem to be just so...hard, or just so... scary, or just so... new... OR just so unexpectedly wonderful!
From waking up early, to her first day of school and making new friends - it's a day of discovery and perspective for a little girl named Lizzy.

ISBN 9780997085105
[Juvenile Fiction – ages 4-8]
Printed in the USA by Worzalla, Stevens Point Wisconsin
Typography: Museo, Chalkduster, Cooper, Bauhaus, American Typewriter
The illustrations were done with pen & ink on bristol board, with backgrounds painted in acrylic on canvas or masonite.
Spot colors and finish work created in photoshop. Etcha-sketch was not used in any form, nor were any animals harmed in the creation of this book of fiction.

Brenda Faatz has an undeniable connection with children. Some say it's because they instinctively know "one of their own." A graduate of The University of Northern Colorado with a degree in Musical Theatre, Brenda is a professional singer, dancer and actor. Along with her husband, Peter Trimarco, she wrote the music, lyrics and script for the original *Wee Noteables* musical theatre live performance series for children. Brenda also founded and directs the *Notable Kids Arts Center* in Denver, Colorado where she has the honor of interacting with and learning from children and their families on a daily basis. This is her first children's book because, as she likes to say... "no one ever told me I couldn't."

Peter Trimarco was a fine arts student who graduated from Lake Forest College with a degree in literature and went on to pursue a career as an editorial cartoonist and commercial artist. Before being inspired by the opportunity to co-write and illustrate a children's book with Brenda, he journeyed through life as an entertainment industry professional. From art director to executive producer to co-founder and publisher of an international film magazine, he realized a good deal of success (awards and working with people who had entourages). But then came working with children, inspiring a new and worthy passion. The words began to flow and with it, the paint, the ink and, most important, the orange hair on Lizzy's head.
...and three simple words from Brenda put it all in motion" "It's Just So..."

For more information on "It's Just So..." books and free coloring pages, visit us at:
Itsjustso.net or NotableKidsPublishing.com